THE HOLIDAY EXPRESS

by

Janice L. McDermott, LCSW, M.Ed.

ISBN 978-1-969865-93-0 (Paperback)
ISBN 978-1-969865-94-7 (Ebook)

Inquiries and Book Orders should be addressed to:

Leavitt Peak Press
17901 Pioneer Blvd Ste L #298,
Artesia, California 90701
Phone #: 2092191548

DEDICATED

To

My grandchildren

Christopher, Anna, and Jack O'Donnell

And their children

THE HOLIDAY EXPRESS

"What is a holiday?' Jack asked Anna his seven-year-old sister.

"A holiday is a special day like your birthday" Anna explained in her most assertive voice…"And no one goes to school or work!"

Jack thought for a moment…then excitedly says, "like every day at bedtime is a special time for stories, we can have a special holiday every day, too."

"Not every day," smiles grandmama, waiting to tell them their bedtime story. "Holidays are special days for everyone at the same time, like New Years Eve when people all over the world are excited together, and on holidays we do fun things with people we love."

"Can we have our special story time, now?" Asks Anna, in her most polite voice and her biggest smile as she and her brother settle into bed.

"Ok", says, Grandmama. "Each of you give me two words to use in our *'One and Only Bedtime Story'.*"

"Trains and ghost," says Jack.

"Bunnies and parades," responds Anna.

Everyone gets quiet as the story begins…

The Holiday Express

LOOK OUT! The Holiday
Express is whizzing by,
It's traveling Eastward in the dark night sky.

The engine roars and puffs out smoke.
Listen now this is not a joke!
The train speeds fast along the track,
Hear that, "Clicked-clicked-clack."

Chasing the engine is the Easter car,
Yellow and pink with a bright gold star.
Loaded with goodies and candies to munch,
Chocolate bunnies? Oh, yes,
there's a BUNCH!
In the corner is the Easter Bunny,
Painting the eggs with sticky honey.
Baskets stuffed, and sure to please,
With paper grass up to our knees.
Big white bunnies, yellow chicks, too!
WOW! Can this be the big city zoo?
No! That's the Easter car that just passed.
This Holiday Express is moving too fast!

The next car that we can see
Parades our Statue of Liberty.

"Hot dogs, watermelon and ice cream,
All for the 4th of July!" they scream.
"Get your cotton candy and snow cones, now!"
Oh! My tummy mumbles, grumbles and growls.
We keep our cool drinking lemonade,
And watch the bands march in parade.
Music and fireworks on display,
Lip-sync contests make our day.
Flags are waving from morning to night.
Our country's birthday is quite a sight!

FREE
Lemonade

OH, NO! OH, MY! What do I see?
A scary car comes right at ME!
Moans and screams pour out from inside.
Someone is taking a scary, ride!
Say, "TRICK OR TREAT" for that's the code
To open the doors on this carload.

EEEE

A peek inside soon reveals...
Vampire coffins, all unsealed.
Lots of ghosts dancing on the walls,
And black cats sharpening their claws.

Big orange pumpkins sleeping by the door,
Witches' eyeballs rolling on the floor.
A spider web and big spiders too,
Just waiting to DROP on top of you!

Hang on now, no need to fear
Kinfolks are arriving here.

See, the next car very close behind,
Grandma 'n Grandpa coming to dine.
A car full of relatives with lots of food,
Laughing and singing, and all in a good mood.

JAM

Cakes, pies and a turkey, WOW!
Yes, Thanksgiving time is right now.
Lots of cousins, and uncles and aunts
Eating so much they pop their pants.

Then a car full of toys, filled to the top,
Each one is handmade in Santa's *own* shop.
Look! There in the car is Santa himself
Playing hide 'n seek with his favorite elf.

The Holiday Express speeds on by,
The last two cars cross the night sky.
A sleigh full of reindeer,
one nose that glows,
"Who's been naughty or nice?"
Only Santa knows.

2025

The Holiday Express passes out of sight
Disappearing into the morning light
Remember to listen when stars first appear
For the Holiday Express is soon coming near.

THE END